Hello, Nittany Lion!

Aimee Aryal

Illustrated by Livio Ramondelli
Penn State, Class of 2004

MASCOT BOOKS

www.mascotbooks.com

It was a beautiful fall day
at Penn State.

The Nittany Lion was on his way to
Beaver Stadium to watch a football game.

He passed in front of Old Main.

A professor walking by waved,
"Hello, Nittany Lion!"

He walked by the Nittany Lion Inn
and over to the Nittany Lion Shrine.

A couple passing by said,
"Hello, Nittany Lion!"

The Nittany Lion walked by the
Pattee and Paterno Libraries.

Some students on the steps yelled,
"Hello, Nittany Lion!"

The Nittany Lion stopped at the
Creamery to get an ice cream cone.

A family sitting outside waved,
"Hello, Nittany Lion!"

It was almost time for the football game.
As the Nittany Lion ran to the stadium,
he passed by some alumni.

The alumni remembered the Nittany Lion
from when they went to Penn State.
They said, "Hello, again, Nittany Lion!"

Finally, the Nittany Lion arrived
at Beaver Stadium.

As he ran onto the football field, the Nittany Lion cheered, "Let's Go, State!"

The Nittany Lion watched the game from
the sidelines and cheered for the team.

Penn State scored six points!
The quarterback shouted,
"Touchdown, Lions!"

At half-time the Blue Band
performed on the field.

The Nittany Lion and the crowd sang,
"Fight on State."

The Penn State Nittany Lions
won the football game!

The Nittany Lion gave Coach Paterno
a high-five. The coach said,
"Great game, Nittany Lion!"

After the football game, the
Nittany Lion was tired. It had been
a long day in Happy Valley.

He walked home and climbed into bed.

"Goodnight, Nittany Lion."

For Anna and Maya, and all of the
Nittany Lion's little fans. ~ AA

For my family, for always being there for me,
and to the biggest lion I know — my cat Nito. ~ LR

Special thanks to:

Andy Dolan

Derek Lochbaum

Joe Paterno

Brian and Tara Swensen

For information please contact Mascot Books,
P.O. Box 220157, Chantilly, VA 20153-0157.

THE PENNSYLVANIA STATE UNIVERSITY, PENN STATE, NITTANY LIONS,
NITTANY LION, PSU, BLUE BAND and the NITTANY LION INN
are registered trademarks of The Pennsylvania State University.

ISBN: 0-9743442-9-X

Printed in the United States.

www.mascotbooks.com

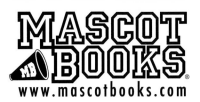

www.mascotbooks.com

MLB

Boston Red Sox
Hello, Wally!
by Jerry Remy

New York Yankees
Let's Go, Yankees!
by Yogi Berra

New York Mets
Hello, Mr. Met!
by Rusty Staub

St. Louis Cardinals
Hello, Fredbird!
by Ozzie Smith

NFL

Dallas Cowboys
How 'Bout Them Cowboys! by Aimee Aryal

NBA

Coming Soon

NHL

Coming Soon

Collegiate

Auburn University
War Eagle! by Pat Dye
Hello, Aubie! by Aimee Aryal

Boston College
Hello, Baldwin! by Aimee Aryal

Brigham Young University
Hello, Cosmo!
by Pat and LaVell Edwards

Clemson University
Hello, Tiger! by Aimee Aryal

Duke University
Hello, Blue Devil! by Aimee Aryal

Florida State University
Let's Go 'Noles! by Aimee Aryal

Georgia Tech
Hello, Buzz! by Aimee Aryal

Indiana University
Let's Go Hoosiers! by Aimee Aryal

Louisiana State University
Hello, Mike! by Aimee Aryal

Michigan State University
Hello, Sparty! by Aimee Aryal

Mississippi State University
Hello, Bully! by Aimee Aryal

North Carolina State University
Hello, Mr. Wuf! by Aimee Aryal

Penn State University
Hello, Nittany Lion! by Aimee Aryal

Purdue University
Hello, Purdue Pete! by Aimee Aryal

Rutgers University
Hello, Scarlet Knight!
by Aimee Aryal

Syracuse University
Hello, Otto! by Aimee Aryal

Texas A&M
Howdy, Reveille! by Aimee Aryal

UCLA
Hello, Joe Bruin! by Aimee Aryal

University of Alabama
Roll Tide! by Kenny Stabler
Hello, Big Al! by Aimee Aryal

University of Arkansas
Hello, Big Red! by Aimee Aryal

University of Connecticut
Hello, Jonathan! by Aimee Aryal

University of Florida
Hello, Albert! by Aimee Aryal

University of Georgia
How 'Bout Them Dawgs!
by Vince Dooley
Hello, Hairy Dawg! by Aimee Aryal

University of Illinois
Let's Go, Illini! by Aimee Aryal

University of Iowa
Hello, Herky! by Aimee Aryal

University of Kansas
Hello, Big Jay! by Aimee Aryal

University of Kentucky
Hello, Wildcat! by Aimee Aryal

University of Maryland
Hello, Testudo! by Aimee Aryal

University of Michigan
Let's Go, Blue! by Aimee Aryal

University of Minnesota
Hello, Goldy! by Aimee Aryal

University of Mississippi
Hello, Colonel Rebel!
by Aimee Aryal

University of Nebraska
Hello, Herbie Husker! by Aimee Aryal

University of North Carolina
Hello, Rameses! by Aimee Aryal

University of Notre Dame
Let's Go Irish! by Aimee Aryal

University of Oklahoma
Let's Go Sooners! by Aimee Aryal

University of South Carolina
Hello, Cocky! by Aimee Aryal

University of Southern California
Hello, Tommy Trojan!
by Aimee Aryal

University of Tennessee
Hello, Smokey! by Aimee Aryal

University of Texas
Hello, Hook 'Em! by Aimee Aryal

University of Virginia
Hello, CavMan! by Aimee Aryal

University of Wisconsin
Hello, Bucky! by Aimee Aryal

Virginia Tech
Yea, It's Hokie Game Day!
by Cheryl and Frank Beamer
Hello, Hokie Bird! by Aimee Aryal

Wake Forest University
Hello, Demon Deacon!
by Aimee Aryal

West Virginia University
Hello, Mountaineer! by Aimee Aryal

Road Races

Marine Corps Marathon
Run, Miles, Run! by Aimee Aryal

Crim Festival of Races
Running Bear and the Crim Kids!
by Su Nottingham

Visit us online at www.mascotbooks.com for a complete list of titles.